Raft Island Treasure Hunters

DJ Quinn

Published by DJ Quinn

Copyright © 2024 by DJ Quinn

All rights reserved.

No part of this publication may be reproduced, distributed, or transmitted in any form or by any means, including photocopying, recording, or other electronic or mechanical methods, without the prior written permission of the publisher, except as permitted by U.S. copyright law.
For permission requests, contact publisher DJ Quinn.

This story fictitious. No identification with actual persons (living or deceased) is intended or should be inferred.

Illustrations by Richard Lehman, Seattle WA

Book Cover by GetCovers.com

First Edition

Paperback IBSN: 979-8-9893174-4-8

eBook IBSN: 979-8-9893174-3-1

Dedication

In honor of Ed.

*A great neighbor, a wonderful friend,
and apparently a fantastic bear hunter.*

Contents

Raft Island Treasure Hunters

1.	Ghost Stories	3
2.	Brush Cutter	5
3.	Raft Island Moonlight	9
4.	The Hunt Is On	13
5.	Into The Forest	19
6.	The Treasure Trail	22
7.	Dead Man's Island	27
8.	Beluga	32
9.	The Haunted Island	36
10.	Beach Shadows	43
11.	Fred Stinger's Story	49

12.	Potato Pancakes	56
13.	Unlocking The Secret	64
14.	The Treasure Of Raft Island	67
Acknowledgements		73
About the Author		75
About the Illustrator		76

Once Upon A Time...

Once upon a time, two brothers and their grandparents traveled to Raft Island, a magical place that was far, far away. The small island was tucked away in a quiet spot on Washington's Puget Sound. On summer days, sunshine would glitter on the salt water and send sparkles of light onto the houses and cabins along the shoreline.

Then the tide would shift, and the sun would drop behind the Olympic Mountains. As the sun disappeared, the sky turned pitch-black and the heavens filled with twinkling stars. Out in the deep water, seals splashed and the barking sound of sea lions echoed.

The forest filled with the sounds of hooting owls and wild animals rustled in the brush. Then in the darkness, the moment arrived when the magic of Raft Island came to life...

1
Ghost Stories

GRANDMA BECKY WAS CRYING, but she wasn't sad. No, Grandma Becky was crying because she was laughing so hard. She was laughing about what happened to Fred Stinger when the bear attacked. Witten was sure that if Grandma Becky laughed any harder, she was going to poop her pants just like Fred Stinger pooped his!

Tonight was their first night on Raft Island, and Kannon and Witten loved it. The two brothers were huddled with their grandparents around a small campfire on Uncle Dennis' beach. The sky was pitch black and filled with a gazillion tiny stars. The moon was making spooky shadows on the top of the water. As the boys roasted marshmallows, they watched for sea creatures in the moonlit water. They were listening to Uncle Dennis and Uncle Joe tell wonderful legends about Raft Island.

In the glow of the campfire, the stories made the dark forest behind them come alive. A twig snapped, and Witten edged closer to Papa. He wanted to be safe if a raccoon came near the fire to steal marshmallows. Kannon was keeping one ear tuned to the breeze. He was ready to run if he heard voices chanting, *"If the log breaks..."*

But then Uncle Dennis told the story about the night Fred Stinger went bear hunting. The boys, their grandparents, and the uncles all started laughing real hard. Nobody by the campfire was scared anymore. Who could be scared when you were laughing about Fred Stinger?

"What happened to the bear?" Papa asked. Uncle Dennis didn't know. Nobody knew where the bear went that night. But everybody knew where Fred Stinger went. Fred went straight to the bathroom to clean up!

Kannon grabbed the last two marshmallows and pitched one to his brother. The marshmallow flew past Witten's head into the darkness, heading toward the spot where their uncles' dogs Margo and Montana lie on the beach. The marshmallow bounced off Margo's head and into Montana the Malamute's quick, snapping jaw. Witten was mad and was about to shove Kannon when he noticed their uncles weren't laughing anymore. They looked serious.

"We forgot a story," Uncle Joe whispered. "Tell them Dennis. Tell them about the pirate. Tell them about Brush Cutter."

2
Brush Cutter

Brush Cutter was a famous pirate. Long before many people lived on Raft Island, the island was Brush Cutter's favorite hideout. The small island had a few cabins built near the shore, but the center of the island was a thick forest. The island was filled with huge trees, and a few paths snaked through the thick brush that covered the ground.

Brush Cutter was tall, tan as chocolate, and mean. His black beard was full of knots and hid the scars that were on his jaw. Brush Cutter's brown pirate pants were always dirty, but he wore a clean white shirt, a red scarf and a torn black pirate hat. It was easy to tell Brush Cutter from the other pirates because he didn't have a left hand. Instead, a rusty, razor-sharp machete was attached to the end of his arm. Brush Cutter used the machete to slash anything or anybody who got in his way. In fact, one day when he was mad, he cut down a tall pine tree with a single swing of his machete!

Because he was so fierce, Brush Cutter got very rich robbing ships that were sailing to Seattle. The pirate and his men would follow the ships and attack them at night. After they stole all the gold and jewels, they would set the captured ship on fire. Then they would sail to their hideout on Raft Island and bury the stolen treasure.

Brush Cutter owned one of the first houses on Raft Island. It was a brick house built right on the edge of Million Dollar Beach. From his house, Brush Cutter could see any ships approaching to capture him. When he wasn't at sea, Brush Cutter would sit on the deck of his house with his feisty girlfriend Beluga. Together they would daydream about the day when they might have as many real dollars as there were sand dollars lying in front of them on Million Dollar Beach.

Brush Cutter never slept in his house at night because he might be captured there. Every night, Brush Cutter snuck away to his 'bedroom', a tiny tree house hidden deep in the jungle-like forest of Raft Island. The tree house was made from rough wood and was covered with green pine branches for camouflage. It had short walls with huge posts on each corner that held up a pointed wood roof. Brush Cutter loved the short walls because they let Raft Island moonlight into the tree house. Brush Cutter believed that if the moon was shining on him, he would be blessed with good luck.

Each night Brush Cutter slept peacefully in the tree house on a soft blanket made of raccoon hides. His dog and cat cuddled nearby, snoring along with him. Then one moonless night, the pirate's luck turned from good to bad. In the darkness, three Navy ships arrived at Raft Island. Sailors came ashore and invaded Brush Cutter's house to capture him.

The sailors woke up Beluga, and she was furious! Beluga fought the sailors fiercely, attacking them with two heavy black frying pans. As the sailors ducked for cover, Beluga screamed. In the chaos, Brush Cutter's parrot flew to the tree house to warn the pirate.

The sailors woke up Beluga, and she was furious!

"*Danger!*" the parrot squawked. "*Danger, Danger!*" Brush Cutter jumped over a wall and out of the tree house. He ran through the thick woods to the other side of the island. In the darkness, he jumped into the cold salt water and swam as fast as he could away from Raft Island. When Brush Cutter reached the opposite shore he disappeared into the darkness.

The sailors captured Beluga, and Beluga ranted and raved. But Beluga would not tell them where Brush Cutter had buried the treasure.

"To this day, the treasure has never been found." Uncle Dennis whispered. "Nor has Brush Cutter the pirate. Many folks are sure that Brush Cutter is still roaming free in the forests near here. People say Brush Cutter is waiting for a summer night with a full moon for good luck. Then he will come out of the forest and steal a boat. He will sneak back to Raft Island to dig up the treasure."

"In fact," Uncle Dennis continued, " searchers still look for Brush Cutter every day. Whenever he's spotted, they put up big orange signs along roads that warn drivers to look out for BRUSH CUTTER AHEAD."

3

Raft Island Moonlight

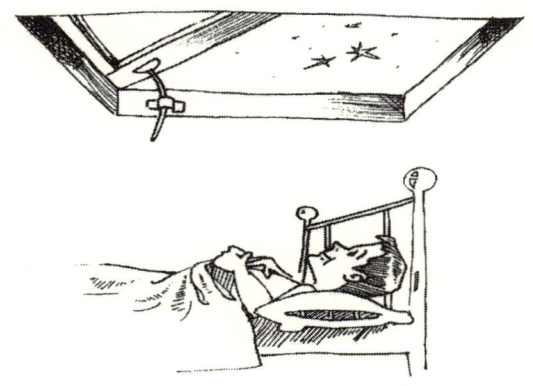

"To this day, the treasure has never been found," Uncle Dennis had said. "Nor has Brush Cutter the pirate."

Kannon couldn't sleep. As the breeze rustled the trees beside the Captain's Quarters, the story kept echoing in Kannon's mind. The treasure—Brush Cutter's treasure—it was still out there, hidden someplace right here on Raft Island!

Kannon looked at the skylight in the ceiling over his bed. In his bedroom at home he had glow-in-the-dark stars glued to the ceiling. At night after a story and prayers, Papa would turn out the lights and the world would get dark. The only light left would be the twinkle of Kannon's fake stars on the ceiling. As Kannon drifted off to sleep, the stars would lose their brightness and fade off to dreamland with him.

On this night, Kannon was sleeping in the Captain's Quarters above the garage at the home of Uncle Dennis and Uncle Joe. There weren't any fake stars here. On Raft Island all the stars were real. From his soft feather pillow, Kannon looked up and saw a sky full of real stars framed in the skylight. Suddenly, he noticed the moonlight shining through the skylight. Kannon was completely covered in Raft Island moonlight!

It was a night where neither the stars above Raft Island nor Kannon faded off to dreamland. Kannon decided that he was going to find Brush Cutter's treasure during this visit to Raft Island. He knew that the moonlight could mean only one thing. It meant he was going to be lucky, and he would find Brush Cutter's treasure!

There was a rustle of blankets as Witten rolled over in his sleep. His little brother—how could that kid sleep on a night like this, Kannon wondered? Brush Cutter's treasure could be anywhere, even right here in the uncles' yard. How could Witten possibly sleep? What was going on inside his little brother's head?

***

Margo couldn't move. Witten pulled and he pushed, but Margo was stuck. All she did was bark her stupid high pitched, "Yap, yap, yap!" The dumb blond dog was covered in stinky mud, and all she could do was bark. It didn't matter that she had a bath today. Tonight, Margo looked like a furry squished up Oreo cookie, and she smelled like a pack of stinky dead seals.

"Hey kid, get off of my beach!" a voice roared behind him. Witten knew who it was, but was too scared to look. "Get moving before I come down there!"

"Come on Margo!" Witten yelled, trying again to pull her from the mud. "We gotta move!"

The old blond dog just looked at him. She was too cute to care about moving. Margo loved getting all muddy on Million Dollar Beach, and she couldn't understand why this boy wasn't having fun in the mud like every other kid that came here. Witten had brought Margo here at low tide to look for something, and he kept telling her to dig. So she dug and dug, making a huge, deep hole. It was turning into a pit that would soon swallow both her and the frantic kid.

"I said to beat it!" The man's loud voice was closer, just a few feet behind them. Witten heard the mud go squish, squish, squish as the man's steps came closer.

Witten pulled as hard as he could. Suddenly a big colorful parrot flew right over his head.

"Danger, Danger!" the parrot squawked. *"DANGER!"* The footsteps got closer. Witten was terrified. He yanked the leash and Margo started to wiggle in the mud. Bit by bit, she pulled free.

Suddenly there was a flash! Witten screamed as Brush Cutter's rusty machete slashed down through the moonlight. The machete sliced Margo's leash, cutting it just inches from where Witten was holding the leash. Then a hand squeezed Witten's shoulder and shook him fiercely.

"Stop!" the voice commanded. "Stop screaming!"

Witten tried to scream again, and a pillow was thrown over his face.

"Stop it, Witten! You'll wake up Grandma Becky and Papa!"

The voice was different. It wasn't Brush Cutter's voice. It was Kannon.

"Wake up! What's wrong with you?" Kannon hissed.

Witten couldn't answer. He tried to rub the sleep out of his eyes but was blinded by all the moonlight shining through the skylight. Witten realized he wasn't on the muddy beach with Margo. He was safe inside the Captain's Quarters. His adventure with Margo on Million Dollar Beach had been just a dream. Witten took a deep breath. He knew he was safe, and he felt very lucky.

4

The Hunt Is On

THE NEXT MORNING BOTH boys were groggy, so Grandma Becky and Papa let them hang out in bed. Their grandparents went next door to have coffee with Uncle Dennis and Uncle Joe.

As soon as the door clicked shut behind their grandparents, Kannon and Witten sprang out of bed. They weren't sleepy. They were ready to talk about the night before. The boys talked about Brush Cutter, about the treasure, and about Witten's dream. They both agreed that last night's moonlight was going to bring them good luck. As sunbeams started to sprinkle down from the skylight, the boys planned. They would use the rest of their vacation for a treasure hunt. Together they would find Brush Cutter's treasure.

The boys heard the door to the Captain's Quarters swing open. An energetic voice yelled up the stairs.

"Who wants to go check the crab trap?" Uncle Joe hollered. "I'm heading out if you want to come."

The brothers flew off the bed and dashed down the stairs. They loved paddling out in the rowboat to pull up the trap. The crab trap was always full of crab, starfish and other little creatures from the bottom. Maybe today the boys would even pull up a clue about where the treasure was hidden!

The white plastic rowboat wobbled as Uncle Joe pulled on the small wooden paddles. Kannon had his eyes peeled looking for any place that Brush Cutter might have stashed the treasure. Witten wasn't helping Kannon look; in fact, he wasn't looking for anything. Witten was yacking away, asking Uncle Joe a million questions as he rowed, and Uncle Joe answered them all.

"No, he had never met Beluga. Yes, some cranky old woman lived in Brush Cutter's house. Yes, it could be Beluga. No, he wasn't 100% sure it was her. No, they couldn't go ask her about the treasure because her dogs chased people. No, the spider in the rowboat wasn't poisonous. Yes, Brush Cutter's tree house was still standing. No, they couldn't go search the tree house because some kids used it as their clubhouse..."

The questions kept flying as they reached the crab trap. Kannon tugged on the rope, then pulled and pulled. The trap rose slowly to the surface and it was loaded. Inside two big crabs were frantically trying to escape. A huge, slimy starfish was stuck on the bottom, and four tiny crabs scampered around the edges. Uncle Joe carefully reached in, nabbed the small crabs, and handed them to the boys. It was time for a round of Olympic Crab Toss.

"Let 'er rip!" Witten screamed as he and Kannon tossed the small crabs into the air. They pitched them as far as they could, sending the little crabs on a quick flight to freedom that ended with a splash into the water.

Uncle Joe was excited because the two big crabs were 'keepers' and would be dinner. But the boys were disappointed. The crab trap might have caught dinner, but didn't help them find what they were looking for—some clues to the treasure.

The large red crabs kept clawing at the bucket trying to escape as the rowboat bobbled back to shore. Kannon was deep in thought, trying to make a new plan. Uncle Joe was once again busy answering questions from Witten.

"No, I don't think it was Brush Cutter who slashed off the biggest crab's front claw. Yes, it could have been bitten off by a fish. No, it was not a shark. Yes, I'm sure the treasure is here on Raft Island right now..."

"Look!" Kannon yelled, interrupting his brother's non-stop questioning. "Over there—by that log!" The rowboat almost tipped as Witten and Uncle Joe turned to look. A quick glance and they saw what Kannon was excited about. Above the rock-covered beach a large log stuck out from the eroded shoreline. The log trailed to a pointed edge several feet out on the beach. Near the pointed end, a partially buried glass bottle with a cork in it was poking up from the mud.

As soon as they reached shore, Kannon and Witten jumped out and splashed their way over to the bottle. Uncle Joe smiled at the boys' excitement, then grabbed the crabs and headed up the hill. Tonight's dinner was squirming in his hands, desperately trying to escape before Uncle Joe reached the kitchen.

Only the top of the bottle was visible on the beach. It had been uncovered when the tide went out that morning. The brothers knelt and worked together to dig the gray mud away from the bottle. Gently they pulled the filthy bottle from its hiding spot and ran to the water to wash their discovery. When the mud fell from the side of the bottle, their hearts skipped a beat. There was something inside! Kannon tried to pry the cork free, but it was stuck.

"Let me try!" Witten yelled, trying to wrestle the bottle from his brother. "I can do it!"

"Bet you can't open it," Kannon said. He poked the cork one more time, then handed the bottle to his brother.

Witten tugged on the cork, then pushed. The cork didn't move. He tried again, but no luck. Suddenly he threw the bottle as hard as he could at a big rock on the beach. SMASH!

"Bet I could!" Witten yelled as glass flew everywhere. He had a smirk on his face.

Their hearts skipped a beat. There was something inside the bottle!

The paper that was inside the bottle rested on the beach, surrounded by shattered glass. Kannon grabbed the paper, took a quick look, and yelled.

"Look! A map!" The paper was worn and ripped, but it was clearly an old map. Years in the bottle had made it hard to read, but they were sure of what they had found.

"It's Brush Cutter's treasure map!" Witten screamed. The boys sat on a log and studied the map together. The yellow paper was brittle and some of the ink was smeared. One edge was charred, and the boys could tell by looking that part of the map was missing.

"I bet Brush Cutter burned it," Witten exclaimed. "He burned the map. He was trying to keep the hiding spot of the treasure a secret!"

The boys stared at the map for clues. There were simple drawings, and a dotted trail snaked on and off the burnt edge several times. Along the edges were pictures of stick people, some of them wearing headbands with feathers. There were raccoons, birds, and fish sketched on the map, plus a drawing of a bear in the center. The sun and moon were pictured, with moonlight shown falling on two stick figures—one tall, one short. All along the edges were trees, with more trees drawn along the trail as it crossed into the burned portion of the map. The dotted trail stayed inside a crooked line on the map.

"That means it's an island," Kannon said after a few seconds. "That crooked line is where the shore of the island goes." But something was missing—there was no X to mark the location of the treasure.

"We're going to have to figure out the clues to find it," Witten said, sounding frustrated. "Since there is no X on the map, the treasure must be hidden on the part that was burned off."

Kannon folded the map carefully and tucked it into his pocket. The boys knew they were lucky, and also knew they would soon be rich! Before they left the beach, they made a pact. They would not tell anyone about the map and would keep their treasure hunt a secret. They would surprise Grandma Becky and Papa and their uncles AFTER they found Brush Cutter's treasure!

5
Into The Forest

After studying the map, Kannon and Witten decided their best bet was to go search in the forest and find the path to the treasure. Yesterday while walking Margo and Montana with Uncle Joe, they had spotted a place they wanted to explore. The boys wanted to investigate a mysterious trail they had seen. The trail seemed to disappear into the forest near Chuck The Waterman's house. They had a hunch it just might be the trail on the map, the one that would lead them to the treasure.

Huge trees hung over Raft Island Drive at the entrance to the forest. The trees made a tunnel of pine branches that swallowed the road, making visitors feel they weren't welcome. Inside the tunnel of trees it was dead quiet. Other than the occasional sound of snarling raccoons or screaming eagles, nothing made a sound. It was a perfect place for Brush Cutter to hide his treasure.

They were brave boys, but not brave enough to explore the forest alone. So the brothers decided to take Margo and Montana with them. The dogs could help them search and would keep them safe. That evening while Grandma Becky and Papa were busy talking with the uncles, Kannon asked if he could take the dogs and his little brother on a walk.

Margo and Montana were excited to go! They were both getting old, but still loved to go for a walk. Once they were out of the yard, the brothers were in a hurry to get to the forest. But the dogs could care less about the forest. Margo would prance a couple steps, then stop to sniff bushes. Montana trotted ahead and wandered into every neighbor's yard looking for treats. The dogs were in no rush.

Suddenly things got scary. Both dogs scampered to the edge of the road and disappeared into a yard marked by a sign with the owner's name. STINGER! Margo and Montana were now messing about in the yard of Fred Stinger, the famous Raft Island bear hunter!

Suddenly there was a roar!

Kannon and Witten called the dogs to come back, but Margo and Montana ignored them. Montana was on a mission. He ran as fast as he could, made a flying leap, and knocked over Fred Stinger's garbage can. As Montana chomped happily at the 'Bad Dog Buffet', Margo decided to have some fun digging in Fred Stinger's vegetable garden.

Suddenly there was a roar! It sounded like a bear, but it wasn't. It was Fred Stinger! He was chasing Margo and Montana out of his yard with a broom and a whole bunch of naughty words!

The boys sprinted up the road, and the dogs flew past them. All of them hightailed it toward the forest. Fred Stinger had chased Montana and Margo before. They knew not to mess with the famous bear hunter. Kannon and Witten followed the dogs through the tunnel of trees. With Fred Stinger hot on their tail, they entered a place that even Fred Stinger was afraid of. The treasure hunters dashed through the trees into the dark, scary forest of Raft Island.

6

The Treasure Trail

Montana was the first to reach the entrance to the Treasure Trail. The energetic dog had been down this trail many times trying to sneak up on the raccoons that walked through the thick forest on their way to the water. The entrance to the trail was hidden by overgrown ferns and thorny blackberry bushes, but it became a well-worn path a few feet off the road. The path dropped off the side of Raft Island Road and snaked into the trees, leading right into the darkest, most deserted part of the forest.

Witten had made a secret plan to get the dogs to help them find the treasure. He reached into his pants pocket and pulled out two crumpled dollar bills and some coins. He carefully unfolded the bills, called the dogs to him, then let Margo and Montana sniff the money. His plan was simple—let the dogs get the scent of the money, then once they picked up the scent of money, the dogs would follow it right to Brush Cutter's hidden treasure. Margo and Montana would sniff out the treasure and make the brothers rich!

Both dogs were interested in Witten's money. They sniffed the cash. They sniffed it again, and started barking wildly and wagging their tails. Margo and Montana had picked up a scent, and Witten was sure his clever plan was working!

But Witten forgot that inside his pocket with the money he also had a bunch of candy. What Margo and Montana smelled wasn't money. They smelled candy, and they wanted the candy now! The dogs charged Witten and knocked him into the bushes. They attacked him like two furry monsters, pulling on his pants pocket with their teeth to find some candy.

"Get off! No, bad dog—get off!" Kannon screamed as he charged to the rescue. He chased Margo and Montana off his little brother. When Witten got up, there were weeds sticking out of his hair, and naughty words just like Fred Stinger's were flying out of his mouth! Margo and Montana ran off, heading further down the trail to escape before Witten caught them. The dogs barked as they ran, and Witten charged behind them hollering like a real bear hunter!

The path went down a dip and then up a slight hill. At the top of the hill, the boys could see the glimmer of the water below. The Treasure Trail then led slowly down the hill, looking like it would disappear into the thick blackberry bushes at every bend. Kannon and Witten were positive they were on the very trail Brush Cutter used to hide the treasure. They knew that some moonlit night, Brush Cutter was going to sneak up from the deserted beach below and follow this trail to get his treasure.

The blackberry bushes along the trail were thick and had sharp thorns. There was no way the boys could search for treasure in those bushes. They kept moving along the Treasure Trail toward the water, sure that they would find what they were looking for just up ahead.

When they came around a corner, they saw a horrible sight. There was no deserted beach, no place where Brush Cutter could have come ashore! There were some small cabins built in a circle, and the boys knew they had reached the church camp. The beach near the cabins was nothing but a dark black line of stinky mud, the kind of mud that dropped like quicksand whenever anyone stepped on it.

The boys now knew this wasn't Brush Cutter's Treasure Trail. It was just a trail in the woods made by kids from the church camp.

"Darn it!" Kannon moaned. "Even a strong pirate like Brush Cutter could never walk across that black mud beach without sinking."

The disappointed brothers turned around and began the long walk up the hill. The dogs trotted behind them. A scary silence surrounded them as the evening shadows began to darken everything in the thick, spooky forest.

Just before they reached the road, the bushes moved. Back and forth the branches rustled in the dim light. In the exact spot where the dogs had knocked over Witten, something was crawling around in the bushes! When Margo and Montana started to bark, Kannon saw black fur moving toward them in the bushes.

"A bear!" Kannon screamed. "It's a bear! Run for your life!"

It's a bear! Run for your life!

Kannon's scream scared Witten. It scared Margo and Montana too! It even scared Kannon! The four of them ran as fast as they could to Raft Island Road, out of the tunnel of trees, and zoomed past Fred Stinger's place. They didn't stop running until they were standing at Uncle Dennis' house!

"We're safe!" whispered Witten, huffing and puffing to catch his breath. "We're lucky we didn't get killed!" The boys were both shaking, happy just to be alive!

Back inside the forest, the bear was happy too. But this bear wasn't a real bear. He was a huge black Newfoundland dog named Bear that was visiting the church camp with

25

his human. Bear's favorite game was to explore the forest without being seen by humans. Tonight, he was following a scent to something near the side of the trail, and that was where the brothers saw him.

Right before Bear had scared away the two screaming boys and their dogs, the Newfoundland had picked up a scent. He smelled candy, some candy that had been in a pocket with some money. As the boys and their barking dogs ran away, Bear found his own treasure. He plopped down in the forest, and happily ate all the candy that had fallen out of Witten's pocket when Margo and Montana had knocked him into the bushes.

7

Dead Man's Island

THE NEXT MORNING AT breakfast Uncle Dennis made an announcement. "Today we're going on a picnic," he said. "We're going to load up the boat and go over to Dead Man's Island."

Kannon dropped his spoon and it smashed his cereal bowl. Across the table, Witten stopped chewing and stared.

His eyes were wide, bulging out almost as far as his Cheerio-filled cheeks.

Dead Man's Island! The boys had heard plenty of Raft Island legends from their uncles around the beach fires. But none was scarier than the story of Dead Man's Island. It was called Cutt's Island these days, standing less than a mile away from Raft Island. Uncle Dennis told the boys that people called it Cutt's Island because the real name—Dead Man's Island—frightened them.

You could see Dead Man's Island from Brush Cutter's house on Million Dollar Beach. The island looked like a small cupcake standing out in the water, frosted with tall pine trees on top of massive cliff edges. On clear days, the sun would shine on the trees of Dead Man's Island just before sunset. When that happened, people said that all the trees on the island looked like they were on fire. They burned until the sun dipped below the distant mountains.

Uncle Dennis' legend was that years ago, the Indians would take dead tribe members to Dead Man's Island to give them back to the Great Spirit. Their bodies were taken to the top of the island, placed on pine needles, and left there. It was believed that at sunset, the Great Spirit would return to Dead Man's Island and set the trees on fire. The spirits of the dead would rise to the sky in the smoke and go join the Great Spirit at the Happy Fishing Waters. It was believed it was a sacred event, because when the sun rose next morning all the trees would be green and beautiful again.

Kannon and Witten were excited to go to Dead Man's Island, but they were worried. The boys had done some quick math and figured out that over the years, hundreds of dead bodies were probably left lying around on the island waiting for the Great Spirit to take them fishing. The boys weren't worried at all about the good spirits who had gone up in smoke to the Happy Fishing Waters. But what about the nasty ones, those mean spirits that even the Great Spirit didn't want to fish with? Were they still there? Was Dead Man's Island haunted?

The thought that the small island was haunted scared the boys. But they were still excited to go there, because they knew a brave pirate like Brush Cutter might think that an island haunted by bad spirits was a great place to hide treasure. The boys were now convinced that Brush Cutter had put his treasure out on Dead Man's Island to keep it safe.

***

"It's got to be there!" Witten exclaimed. "The island on the map—it is Dead Man's Island, not Raft Island." The brothers had retreated to the beach to look over the secret map and make a plan. Grandma Becky, Papa, and their uncles were busy in the house getting ready for their trip to Dead Man's Island.

"Think about it Kannon. The stick guys with the feathers—they are Indians." Witten insisted. "Brush Cutter drew them to show he hid the treasure someplace where they hang out waiting for the Great Spearfish to burn the trees so they can go fishing."

"Spirit," Kannon corrected.

"What?" Witten asked.

"He's the Great Spirit, not the Great Spearfish," Kannon explained to his brother.

"Whatever!" Witten was too excited to care about the details.

"And Brush Cutter probably burned the map as a clue! He's trying to show that the Treasure Trail leads to someplace where there's a lot of fire!"

"Maybe the trees caught fire while he was drawing the map and burned it. Brush Cutter had to escape and decided to leave the burn mark on the map for a clue," Kannon said, beginning to catch his little brother's enthusiasm. Witten was probably right—Brush Cutter had fooled everyone. The pirate had hidden his treasure on Dead Man's Island!

"What about that?" Witten asked, pointing to the map. The boys stared at a faint sketch on the map they hadn't noticed before. A drawing of a stick figure with a feather was floating over the trail near the burn. It had a nasty frown drawn on its face. "Do you think Dead Man's Island is haunted?"

"Are you chicken, Witty?" Kannon teased. "Do you want to stay here, and I'll go find the treasure and get rich? Bawk, bawk, bawk! Witty is a wittle chicken!"

Witten gave his brother a shove. Ghosts or no ghosts, he was going to find Brush Cutter's treasure. "Just be careful," he told Kannon. "You never know what we'll find out there."

8
Beluga

As Uncle Joe backed the motorboat away from the shore, Kannon and Witten settled into the seats in the open bow. These were the best seats, ones that gave them a great view of the Raft Island shoreline, Brush Cutter's house, and Dead Man's Island. Grandma Becky, Papa, and Uncle Dennis were in the back with Uncle Joe, meaning the boys were free to make plans without being heard.

"See that A-frame house where the Washington State University flag is flying? A big family of Cougar fans owns that one, and next to that is a little beach park for Raft Island residents. And Mr. Watson used to own that house..."

Uncle Joe was playing tour guide, telling Grandma Becky and Papa stories about the places they passed. Uncle Joe knew everything about Raft Island, but the brothers weren't interested. Their eyes were glued on the only house they cared about. They wanted to get a good look at Brush Cutter's house on Million Dollar Beach.

"There she is!" Witten said in a startled voice. "Look! On that deck! She's right up there!"

Kannon had already seen her. A big woman wearing a pink bathrobe and sandals was waddling around on the sun-covered deck of Brush Cutter's house. She had a cigarette hanging from her mouth and was busy feeding the cats that were crawling all over the deck.

"It's Beluga!" Witten shouted. He nervously squirmed in his seat. "It's her, Brush Cutter's girlfriend!"

The tide was high enough that Uncle Joe was able to drive the boat close to the shore, and they were floating very close to Brush Cutter's house. The boys stared at Beluga as they approached, but the grownups hadn't noticed her yet.

"And we looked at that house too, but it was nasty inside," Uncle Joe the tour guide continued the boat passed a greenish house with a spooky-looking boathouse.

Suddenly her dogs barked, and Beluga stood straight up. She stared at the boat, her powerful black eyes focused right on Kannon and Witten. The boys froze.

"She sees us!" Kannon hissed through clenched teeth. "She's looking right at us!"

Beluga waddled to the end of the deck and glared.

"And there is Brush Cutter's house right there," Uncle Joe said. *'Hey! Look who's up there!"*

The boat horn blasted right behind Kannon's ear as Uncle Joe honked at Beluga. Kannon screamed, dropped his soda over the side of the boat, and ducked for cover on the floor. Witten dove from his seat onto the floor and landed on top of Kannon.

"NO! STOP HONKING! She'll kill us," Witten screamed at Uncle Joe. Both boys were petrified, desperate to escape the evil stare Beluga had locked on the two of them.

From the floor, Witten looked back. He could see Uncle Dennis waving at Beluga. Grandma Becky, Papa, and Uncle Joe were also waving. Witten peeked up over the side and saw that Beluga wasn't moving. She just stood on the deck, staring at the boat.

"I can't breathe!" Kannon gasped from underneath his brother. "Get off me! Get off!"

Kannon squirmed, shoved, and finally managed to push free from under his brother. As the boat floated closer to Brush Cutter's, both boys looked over the side of the boat.

Beluga was standing just a few yards away. She was staring right at them, on the deck puffing her cigarette. Beluga pushed the cats away, then slowly lifted her arm and waved at the boat. The boys gasped, then ducked for cover again.

Beluga was waving all right. She was waving a black frying pan at them. The boys knew it could only mean one thing. Beluga was warning them that they better not mess with her or with Brush Cutter's hidden treasure!

9

The Haunted Island

THE ROCKS AND SAND made a grinding crunch when the boat hit the shore. The boys didn't move, they stood like frozen statues just staring at the clay cliffs ahead of them.

"Abandon ship!" Uncle Dennis commanded. "We're here!"

Here they were at Dead Man's Island, the very last stop for hundreds of dead Indians on their way to the Happy

Fishing Waters. Today they were having a picnic at the place where souls of the dead hung around until they could catch a puff of smoke to ride off into the forever-after. At least that was the story Uncle Dennis told them around the campfire. The brothers wanted to get off the boat, but neither boy could make his feet move.

"Let's go guys," Uncle Joe urged. "Jump out and have a look around."

White shells covered the beach and glistened in the sun as tangled pieces of driftwood cast spooky shadows on the beach. It was dead quiet on the island. Screeching birds and water gently lapping on the beach were the only sounds.

"Go ahead Kannon," Witten urged. "You go first, big brother."

"What a chicken. Bawk, bawk, bawk!" Kannon snorted, giving his brother a shove as he jumped onto the shore behind Uncle Dennis and Papa."

"It takes one to know one!" Witten stood up and hustled out of the boat. "Wait!" he yelled, not wanting to hang out alone on this haunted island. He jumped on the shore and ran to catch up with the group.

"Where shall we eat lunch?" Uncle Dennis asked.

Uncle Dennis was always hungry. They had just stepped onto the beach and Uncle Dennis was ready for lunch. Uncle Joe rolled his eyes and handed Uncle Dennis a cookie.

"Here, have a vitamin," he said. "We'll eat after we explore."

As Uncle Dennis munched on his 'vitamin' they all started a slow walk along the rocky beach. Bits of shells snapped under their feet, and small crabs scampered about looking for places to hide. Both boys had their eyes peeled on the clay cliffs. They knew the trees on top made some great places where Brush Cutter could have hidden his treasure.

"Does this island have any trails?" Kannon asked. "Any trails to the top?"

Uncle Dennis told them that there was a trail up from the other side. The brothers both started to walk faster. This had to be the trail where Brush Cutter had hidden the treasure. Today they would finally find the treasure and be rich!

Kannon and Witten hurried ahead of the slow-moving grownups, stopping occasionally to toss rocks into the sparkling water. When they reached the other side, they were far ahead of Grandma Becky, Papa, and their uncles. Kannon pulled the map out of his pocket and the boys looked at it as they walked, hoping to find the trail to the top.

Suddenly Witten yelled. "Look, above that log!"

It was a trail! A brown dirt path wound up the steep hillside and disappeared into the trees. The brothers dashed to the log, hopped over it, and began the steep climb to the top of Dead Man's Island. The trail wiggled its way through the bushes as it led toward the top of the island. The brush here was much thinner than on Raft Island, making it easy to search for the treasure as they moved along the trail.

"You check that side," Kannon commanded Witten. "I'll look over here." The boys moved quickly along the trail, occasionally scampering off the path to look for treasure in the bushes.

Wham! Witten body-slammed right into his brother, who had come to a dead stop on the trail in the center of the island.

"What are you doing?" Witten yelled.

Kannon didn't move or speak. He was staring at something in the middle of the trail. He looked at Witten and pointed to the charred black remains of what had been a huge bonfire.

"INDIANS!" Witten yelled.

"Shhh!" Kannon whispered. "They might still be here!"

In their excitement to find the trail and treasure, the boys had forgotten all about the dead people. But the sight of the bonfire gave them a spooky reminder that they might not be alone on Dead Man's Island. Kannon backed away a few steps, then led his brother slowly around the spot where the bonfire had been.

"Watch where you walk, Witten. The Great Spirit won't like it if we're stepping all over burned bodies!"

The boys inched along the trail, looking for the treasure with every step. Witten also kept glancing over his shoulder, making sure they weren't being followed. Each time a twig snapped under their feet, the boys got quieter, and their muscles got tighter. Before long, they reached the end of the trail where the cliff overlooked the blue water below.

"Maybe we missed it," Kannon said, pitching a rock off the cliff into the water. "It's got to be here. Let's look again."

"We can look on the way down," Witten said quietly. "We better get back to Grandma Becky and Papa. Let's go." Witten felt creepy. There had been no sign of the treasure on the trail. All they had seen was the fire where dead Indians were burned.

"The little chicken says *bawk, bawk, bawk!*" Kannon teased. It was hard to pass up a chance to bug his little brother. But Kannon felt creepy too. He felt like there might be something else hanging around, something watching them here on top of the island.

Witten led the way, and the boys hurried down the trail without speaking. They glanced occasionally to the sides of the path hoping to spot the treasure, but their focus now was to get back to the beach safely. Suddenly Witten stopped and pointed to a mound of dirt in the trees. It was only a few feet from where the bonfire had been held.

"What?" Kannon whispered. "What do you see?"

Witten was so excited he couldn't talk. He pointed again, then started running toward the mound of dirt. There was something buried there.

"The treasure!" Kannon screamed as he ran after his brother. "We've found the treasure!"

Both boys reached the mound of loose dirt and branches at the same time. They knelt over and began to frantically claw away the loose dirt. Within seconds, Witten hit something with his hand.

The dirt moved. The dirt began to shake, and suddenly a body sprang up from beneath the dirt, shaking free from its shallow grave! The body's face was smeared with black soot, charred from the bonfire that had burned his body. A half-dead Indian jumped out of the grave, looked at the boys and tried to grab them.

"AAHHHGGGG!" the black-faced body bellowed.

The boys screamed bloody murder! They ran as fast as they could down the trail.

"AAHHHGGGG!"

It was chasing them and was getting closer! They scrambled down the hill toward the beach. The Indian's footsteps were right behind them, and he was shrieking at the top of his lungs.

"AAHHHGGGG!" He was coming onto the beach after them! The screaming boys dashed across the beach towards Grandma Becky, Papa, and Uncle Joe.

"Run! Run!" the boys screamed. "An Indian is trying to kill us!" The brothers zipped right past Grandma Becky and Papa and kept running towards the water.

Kannon glanced back to make sure his grandparents were coming. But they weren't, and neither was Uncle Joe. They were all lying on the beach laughing. Kannon slowed and stopped running. When he looked back toward the trail, he saw what was so funny.

"Witten!" he yelled to his brother, who was still hightailing it down the beach. "Witten, look!"

Witten glanced over his shoulder without slowing down. When he realized what was happening he slowed to a walk.

The dirt-covered Indian with the charred face was on the beach walking towards Grandma Becky, Papa, and Uncle Joe. The Indian was laughing hysterically.

The body with the black face wasn't an Indian. It was Uncle Dennis! He had followed the treasure-hunting boys to the top of the island, buried himself in the dirt and waited. When they found him, Uncle Dennis—'the Indian'—had scared the daylights out of the boys.

"That's not funny!" Witten screamed. He was shaking from the scare, but the grownups continued laughing.

Witten and his brother looked at each other. They didn't know for sure if Dead Man's Island was haunted or not. They didn't know where the treasure was hidden. But they did know one thing—they knew Dead Man's Island could be one very, very scary place!

10

Beach Shadows

THE MOON WAS GLISTENING off the smooth, glass-like water. The beach fire was roaring and glowing embers popped from the coals, shooting onto the beach.

"Ugh!" Kannon yelled as a blast of smoke changed direction and whipped into his eyes. He covered his eyes, stumbled to the opposite side of the fire, and squeezed into a space between Uncle Joe and Papa. Uncle Joe was again patiently answering all Witten's questions, which he had been asking non-stop since they left Dead Man's Island.

"Probably not, Witten. No, I've never found a skull on Dead Man's Island. Yes, there probably were bones left after the Great Spirit came to take them fishing. No, we can't take shovels to the island and try to dig up dead Indian bones..."

"Stop it, Witten!" Kannon yelled from across the fire. "Stop asking so many questions!" Kannon needed some quiet time to think. Since they left Dead Man's Island he had been trying to figure out a new plan to find Brush Cutter's treasure. Their vacation was almost over, and the boys still hadn't found where the pirate had hidden his loot.

Yap,yap,yap! Margo's shrill bark pierced the quiet night. Grandma Becky jumped from fright, sending her Diet Coke flying. The ice-cold drink landed on Papa, soaked him, and scared him more than Margo's barking did.

Margo continued to bark without standing up from the comfortable hole she had dug on the beach. Montana was focused and couldn't be bothered by his little blond girlfriend barking at shadows. He was quietly waiting to surprise any raccoon that might stroll by on the beach.

"Hush!" Uncle Joe and Uncle Dennis yelled at the same time. "Margo, HUSH!"

When Margo gave one last yelp, Kannon saw why Margo was barking. A tall, thin shadow was walking in the moonlight on the beach. It approached slowly, creeping carefully around the piers of the neighbor's dock. The shadow passed the dock, moved closer, and quietly stepped along the edge of the water. Kannon knew immediately—the shadowy thing was heading right toward them!

Grandma Becky, Papa, Witten, and the uncles—none of them noticed the shadow sneaking up behind them. Kannon tried to warn them, but he was so scared that he couldn't talk. When the shadow stopped moving, it was standing right behind Grandma Becky.

"Hello!" a voice boomed.

"AAHHHGGGG!" Grandma Becky screamed! The Diet Coke refill Uncle Joe had just given her went sailing into the air. It landed on Witten. He jumped up as ice cubes smacked his head, then he saw the tall shadow standing just inches away from him. Witten screamed, jumped over a log, and bolted down the beach.

Margo and Montana barked when they heard the screams. Montana ran after Witten, took a flying leap, and knocked the terrified kid face-first into the mud. Montana licked the back of his head, wagged his tail, then trotted back to the fire leaving Witten face down in the mud.

"I didn't mean to scare you, sneaking up on you like that," the shadow said, starting to chuckle. "Just thought I'd come over and see what was going on over here."

"Well hello, Fred," Uncle Joe laughed. "Sit down and join us." Everyone was trying to catch their breath as Uncle Joe introduced Papa, Grandma Becky, and Kannon to the shadow. It was Fred Stinger, the famous Raft Island bear hunter!

Kannon couldn't believe it. Here was the famous Fred Stinger sitting right at the beach fire with them. And Stinger was getting a good laugh, knowing he had almost scared the poop out of them when he walked up behind them.

Kannon could tell from the way Fred Stinger had sneaked up on them that he must be one terrific bear hunter. Stinger was tall and wore wire frame glasses on his long, drawn, reddish face. He was wearing a baseball cap over his gray hair, and was dressed in dark clothes. Fred's tennis shoes were so quiet that sneaking up on bears and people was very easy for him.

Uncle Dennis had told the boys that Fred Stinger had lived on Raft Island almost forever. Stinger moved onto the island before Brush Cutter escaped into the forest. Fred lived on Raft Island long before the Raft Island bridge was built, he knew everything about the island, and he knew everybody who lived there.

Fred Stinger knew everything about everyone because he was retired. He spent all his free time finding out what everyone else on Raft Island was doing. Just like tonight, when Fred Stinger was at home busy doing nothing. He told the group around the campfire that he was sitting in his house, *"and then I saw this fire out of my window. I decided dang it all to heck, I'm gonna walk on down there and go look. I'll find out what those stinking Husky fans are up to down there, because they are either causing some trouble or they're having some fun. I think I'll just walk on over there and give them a hard time."*

Kannon thought that Fred Stinger had the friendliest voice he ever heard. Kannon noticed something else—as Fred Stinger sat by the fire talking, Fred was covered in Raft

Island moonlight! Yes, the moon was shining right down on the famous bear hunter.

Suddenly there was a growl! From far away on the beach, a short shadow was running toward the fire swinging a huge stick. The shape was covered in black mud, yelling, and growling like a furious sea monster. As it came closer, the group got a whiff of the monster. It smelled like spilled Diet Coke and stinky beach mud. It was Witten!

"Montana! I'm gonna get you!" Witten was furious. "Come here you dumb dog!"

Montana was excited to play 'chase', so he ran as fast as he could up the hill. Witten was right behind him, screaming at the top of his lungs and swinging the stick. Margo barked furiously, then almost fell right into the fire as she took off after Witten.

Up the hill went Montana. Up the hill went Witten after Montana. Up the hill went Grandma Becky and Papa trying to catch Witten. And up the hill ran Uncle Joe, Uncle Dennis, and Margo, all of them trying to save Montana!

And in the glow of the fire on the beach, Kannon sat with Fred Stinger, listening to Fred tell stories. Fred told Kannon stories about his days as a teacher. Stories about when he was a Washington State Cougar. And best of all, Fred Stinger told stories about Raft Island.

*In the glow of the fire on the beach,
Kannon sat listening to Fred Stinger
tell stories.*

The Raft Island moonlight got brighter as Fred Stinger talked, and now it was shining down on both Kannon and Fred. Kannon noticed the moonlight, and knew that he had been blessed with good luck to be able to talk with Fred Stinger. The moonlight gave him courage, so Kannon reached into his pocket and pulled out the map. Then he asked the famous bear hunter of Raft Island the question he was sure that only Fred Stinger could answer.

"Mr. Stinger, do you know where Brush Cutter hid the treasure?"

11

Fred Stinger's Story

"Oh, that Cutter. You had to watch out for him because he was one mean guy," Fred Stinger told Kannon. "Not the kind of guy I wanted hanging around my place. You know he always acted sort of strange. But I guess I would too if I had a machete for a hand."

The light from the flames danced on Fred Stinger's face as Kannon listened to Stinger's amazing story. Not only had Fred Stinger hunted bears on Raft Island, but Fred had met Brush Cutter the pirate!

"Nobody asked too many questions about the guy, but we all knew he was up to no good. He would sail away for days at a time, then come back and hang out here and never talk to anyone. He'd just sit up on the deck of his house with that goofy girlfriend of his and sharpen that machete for hours and hours. People said that he was taking in a lot of loot from ships. But the guy never spent a dime on anything. So I'm sure that if he did have any money, he was just hiding all of it away."

Hiding it all away! Kannon couldn't believe his ears. Everyone knew that Brush Cutter had robbed lots of ships, but according to Fred Stinger, he never spent what he stole. Wow, there must be a ton of treasure hidden here on Raft Island.

"But where did he hide it?" Kannon asked as he showed Fred Stinger the treasure map. "Do you have any idea where he hid his treasure?"

"Maybe right here," Stinger said while pointing, "but nobody know for sure."

Fred was pointing to a spot on the map, but Kannon saw that Fred Stinger was holding the map upside down. Stinger might have been a great teacher, but he couldn't see worth beans by the firelight. The map was no help tonight. But Fred Stinger didn't need a map because Fred Stinger remembered what he had seen with his very own eyes.

"You see, Cutter was so mean that nobody would even talk with him. Nobody dared to bother him or tried to snoop around looking for where he might be hiding the loot. In fact, Cutter wouldn't even let his own men set foot on Raft Island. They had to stay on their ship or go ashore way out on Key Peninsula when Cutter didn't have them out at sea chasing ships."

"When we were kids, before they put the roads in, we used to roam all over this island," Stinger reminisced. "The forest was thick as glue and it was one scary place, but we loved to play in there. The woods were full of raccoons, deer, and even a mean bear. But the meanest thing running around the forest wasn't a wild animal—it was that danged pirate Brush Cutter! My brother and I were sure that if we ran into him out there in the woods, we'd never make it out alive."

"But we were kids, and we loved exploring. The danger of running into Cutter in the woods made it more exciting. We'd sneak up close to his tree house, the one over there on Park Street, and try to spy on the place. But Cutter always kept his fierce dog inside the tree house. If we got too close the dog would start barking. We'd have to run like the dickens to get home before Cutter caught up with us and chopped us to bits!"

"The last time I saw Cutter was just a couple days before the Navy came after him. It was the strangest thing. My brother and I were walking down the beach to come play in some caves that were here. And who do we run into? Brush Cutter, wearing those filthy brown pants and smelling like smoke. We were shocked to see him because we had been to the caves hundreds of times and never seen any sign of the pirate. He was busy digging in the bushes near the caves, and then he saw the two of us."

"And you know what he did?" Stinger asked. Kannon's eyes were nearly bugging out in amazement from Fred Stinger's story. He couldn't speak—all he could do was shake his head.

Stinger's eyes got really narrow and his face tightened. He leaned forward and spoke in a low, whispered voice. From the other side of the fire, Fred Stinger told Kannon what Brush Cutter did when Fred and his brother discovered the pirate digging near the caves.

"Cutter stared at us with his red bloodshot eyes. He never took his eyes off us, not even for a second. Then Cutter reached down and picked up a raccoon he had caught. The coon was clawing, growling, and scratching the daylight out of Cutter's arm. Then WHACK! With a single slice of his machete arm, Brush Cutter cut off the raccoon's head. Then Cutter reached down, picked up the head, and threw the bloody thing right at my brother and me! It scared the poop right out of us! We knew it was his way of showing us what would happen to us if we messed with him. And believe me, we never went to play in the caves again."

"Was he putting treasure in the caves?" Kannon asked excitedly.

"I never found out," Stinger said with a sigh. "We were so scared that we never came near this part of the beach again. After Cutter disappeared, my brother and I looked all over Raft Island to see if we could find the treasure, but no luck. But we stayed away from this place because that coon head showed us that Cutter really meant business!"

"We were so scared that we never came near this part of the beach again."

"Then years later along comes Scott Dooley, and he decided to build a house here. Scott and his family never knew about the caves, or about Brush Cutter. So Scott was out here digging, plowing dirt, and building. He covered up the caves. I'd wander down every day and look at what was going on, to just poke around a bit. I didn't care about the house, I was looking around to see if they might have uncovered the treasure. But I never found a thing, and neither did Scott."

Suddenly Fred Stinger looked serious. He glanced toward Uncle Joe's house, then back to Kannon. "Can you keep a secret, Kannon? If I tell you something no one knows, can you keep it a secret?" Kannon nodded. He could tell from Fred Stinger's look that the old man had something important to say.

"He came back, Kannon. Brush Cutter—he came back. He was looking for his treasure, and he came back right here to Scott Dooley's house."

Kannon couldn't believe his ears! His heart was pounding as Fred Stinger continued with his secret.

"One night there was a full moon. Scott and Polly and their little girl had just gone to bed. The little girl was sleeping on the first floor, Scott and Polly were in their bedroom upstairs. Scott thought he heard a noise, so he went downstairs to investigate. He looked out all the windows, but there was nothing there. Before he went back upstairs, Scott went to check on his daughter."

"That's when he saw him. There was Brush Cutter, standing outside on the deck, staring in the window. He was wearing his black hat and white shirt, rubbing his knotted black beard. Brush Cutter had come back looking for his treasure! But there was a house built over the spot the caves once were, and he was deciding what to do. That's when he saw Scott looking right at him from inside the house."

"Cutter took one look at Scott, jumped off the deck and ran. He probably didn't want to tip anyone off that he was in the area. Scott grabbed his daughter and ran upstairs. By the time the sheriff came the pirate had vanished. Scott and his family were scared to death. The night that Scott saw Brush Cutter was the first time they had even heard of him. It was also the last night that the Dooleys stayed on Raft Island. They put their house up for sale, and sold it to Dennis and Joe, a couple of city slickers from Seattle who had no clue about pirates or Brush Cutter."

"Nobody has seen Brush Cutter since that night. I bet he is still out in some forest someplace, chopping up raccoons for dinner with that machete, and is just waiting for the right time to come back to Raft Island."

A noise startled Kannon. He jumped up and his heart was pounding when he saw who it was.

"Hi guys! We thought we'd bring down some snacks!" It was Grandma Becky hauling marshmallows to the campfire. His uncles were right behind her.

"Where's Witten?" Kannon asked with an excited voice.

"In bed," Grandma Becky replied. "Papa had him take a shower to clean off and cool down. They are up in the Captain's Quarters settling in for the night."

"And Margo and Montana are in their kennel," Uncle Joe added. "They're wired from having too much fun!"

As Uncle Dennis and Kannon began to set their marshmallow torches on fire, Fred Stinger stood up.

"I better get going before the boss thinks I got lost in the woods and sends out a search party. Plus I'll need to take a bath after being around all you stinking Huskies," Stinger said with a laugh. He turned away, gave a quick wave, then strolled off in the moonlight.

Kannon watched Fred Stinger disappear down the beach. He couldn't wait to tell Witten everything he had learned. The moonlight was very bright, and was shining right on Kannon. He was sure it was a sign that his brother and he were about to be blessed with some very, very good luck!

12

Potato Pancakes

"**Witten, wake up!**" Kannon gave him a shove, trying to get his groggy kid brother to stir without waking Grandma Becky and Papa. "Wake up!"

The sun was beaming into the Captain's Quarters, and Kannon was in a hurry. He hardly slept a wink all night. He kept dreaming about the caves, the treasure, and Brush Cutter. Every time he rolled over, Kannon looked at the window to make sure Brush Cutter wasn't peeking inside.

Luckily, Brush Cutter didn't come back last night and now it was daylight. Kannon needed to wake Witten and get him outside to tell him the story he had heard from Fred Stinger.

"Leave me alone," Witten moaned.

"GET UP!" Kannon hissed. "It's important. It's about Brush Cutter's treasure!"

Witten sprang up in bed, trying to blink the sleep out of his eyes. "What? What about the treasure?"

"Come on!" Kannon whispered as he hauled his brother out of bed. "We're going to the beach."

"Just stay out of the water," Grandma Becky's half-awake voice moaned. Then she rolled over and went back to sleep. Today Papa and Grandma Becky were in no hurry to wake up because Uncle Dennis was going to make potato pancakes for breakfast.

Potato pancakes. The boys didn't really understand, but there was some joke about Uncle Dennis and potato pancakes. The brothers had never had potato pancakes, and they weren't sure if Grandma Becky and Papa had either. Anytime someone mentioned potato pancakes, everyone laughed. But no one admitted to ever eating them.

The boys hurried and got dressed, then headed for the beach. Once they were out the door, Kannon excitedly filled Witten in on Fred Stinger's surprising story.

"Brush Cutter was here!" Kannon exclaimed. "He was looking for the caves to find his treasure and climbed on the deck by the hot tub and scared some girl and the cops came and nobody found the treasure but it's probably right here someplace because once he cut a racoon's head off and warned Fred Stinger to stay away!"

Witten looked at his brother with a blank stare. Kannon was moving way too fast this morning. Witten couldn't make any sense of his excited brother's babble.

"What? Who was here? The raccoons by the hot tub don't have heads?"

"Brush Cutter!" Kannon exclaimed. "The pirate came back and was standing on the deck by the hot tub looking in the windows. And Fred Stinger saw him cut off a racoon's head when Fred saw him burying treasure!"

"Fred Stinger saw a raccoon burying treasure?" Witten asked. He was trying hard to understand what Kannon was talking about, but it was still too early. Kannon let out a sigh, then sat his sleepy brother down on a log on the beach. Slowly, he told Witten the story Fred Stinger had shared with him the night before. Before long, Witten was excited too.

"Brush Cutter came back here? And Fred Stinger really saw him burying treasure?" Witten asked.

"Well, Fred Stinger didn't actually see him burying the treasure. But Brush Cutter was doing something in the bushes and was serious about keeping Fred and his brother away. So he cut the raccoon's head off and threw it at them."

"Wow! Where are the caves? Where he was digging?"

"Let's go ask Uncle Dennis," Kannon suggested. The boys ran up the hill to the house where Uncle Dennis was in the kitchen cooking potato pancakes.

When they walked in the kitchen, the boys understood why potato pancakes were a joke. There were half-peeled potatoes all over the counter. Potato peels were on the floor and in the sink. Uncle Dennis had flour on the counter, in the sink and in his hair. And a pan with nothing in it was smoking on the stove.

"Hi guys!" their happy uncle greeted them as he walked in circles around the kitchen. "Are you hungry?"

"Uncle Dennis, where are the caves? Are they covered up? Do raccoons live in the caves?" Witten asked. Kannon knew his brother was now awake, because his questions were coming at full speed.

"Right over there," Uncle Dennis said as he pointed. WHAP! An egg hit the floor and splattered as Uncle Dennis moved toward the window to show them where the caves used to be. "Near the beach, next to those ferns, there were a bunch of caves. They are covered up now, but you can still see some holes in the ground near where they were."

"Hey, what's burning?" Uncle Joe hollered from upstairs. The smoke from the stove was billowing upstairs, and Uncle Joe was gasping for air.

"Thanks!" the boys yelled. They darted out the door and ran off to find the caves.

***

It was getting hot. The sun was high in the sky and beating down near the boys. Kannon and Witten were digging frantically, making a big pile of dirt stacked next to the hole.

"Remember our deal," Uncle Joe reminded them. "You have to fill the holes back up when you're done digging."

The boys weren't thinking about covering up the holes. They were on the trail of Brush Cutter's treasure. Their digging had led them to what looked like the entrance to a small cave, and they wanted to see if they could uncover the cavern where Brush Cutter had stashed his loot.

Grandma Becky, Papa, and Uncle Joe sat on the beach. Uncle Dennis had chased them all out of the house when the fourth batch of potato pancakes went up in smoke. The kitchen was a mess, everyone was starving, and after all this time there were still no potato pancakes. Everyone was staying away from the house because Uncle Dennis was as mad as a hornet that the potato pancakes kept sticking to the frying pan. The grownups were now waiting on the beach, far away from the chaos of potato pancakes.

The boys kept digging, looking for the treasure. All they had found were two broken bottles, but they weren't discouraged. They had a feeling that today they were going to be lucky.

A screech pierced the morning quiet as the smoke alarm in the kitchen went off! The grownups on the beach looked back just in time to see the latest batch of potato pancakes and the frying pan go flying out the door and over the deck. Then they heard Uncle Dennis in the kitchen cussing like a bear hunter! Flour and potato pieces flew all over the kitchen as he fanned the smoke detector with a towel, trying to stop the beeping. The boys saw Grandma Becky was starting to cry. She was laughing so hard that she, Papa and Uncle Joe fell on the beach laughing.

THUNK! A big rock fell from the side of the hole and hit Witten's shovel. It flipped the shovel out of his hands and shot dirt into Kannon's face.

"Witten!" Kannon yelled, wiping dirt out of his eyes. "Knock it off!"

"Kannon!" Witten screamed. "Kannon--LOOK!" Witten pointed to the side of the hole where the big rock had fallen. There was a hole in the dirt about shoulder high, and there was something resting inside.

Kannon dropped his shovel and scrambled to the hole. Together the boys clawed at the dirt with their hands. There was something in there! It was solid, big, and made of wood.

"I hope it is, I hope it is, I hope it is!" Kannon kept whispering, trying not to get too excited before they were certain of what they had found.

"What is it?" Uncle Joe said from behind them. Uncle Joe had come to tell them to stop digging just as the rock fell. When he saw the box he jumped right into the hole to help the boys. Dirt kept flying as Uncle Joe and the brothers clawed furiously. Bit by bit they uncovered the buried object, an old brown box.

Papa and Grandma Becky came over to watch. When they had moved enough dirt to wiggle the box free, Papa and Uncle Joe pulled it out of the hole and drug it toward the lawn.

The boys began to scream, "IT'S THE TREASURE! WE FOUND THE TREASURE!"

Papa helped the boys wipe off the box, and Uncle Joe ran to get the hose. Their Uncle sprayed the box, and they gathered around it to inspect the boys' discovery. The box was two feet long, one foot high and one foot wide. Rusty brackets on each corner held it together, and two rusty hinges were attached to the lid. It had a big, corroded lock that protected whatever was hidden inside. It had been underground for a long time, and was probably going to be a chore to open.

"Breakfast is ready!" Uncle Dennis shouted from the deck. Everyone was starving, but the brothers didn't want to stop. They wanted to bust open the chest and see what was inside.

"It will take work to get this thing open," Uncle Joe said. "Let's have breakfast, and then I'll help you open it."

The brothers wanted to open it immediately, but Grandma Becky and Papa thought breakfast sounded like a better idea. Over the boys' objections, their grandparents herded them up to the deck for some of Uncle Dennis' famous potato pancakes.

The famished group sat at the table, which was set nicely with orange juice, fruit, coffee and syrup. But the long wait in the sun had wilted the oranges, turned the apples slices brown, and the bananas were pitch black. But nobody cared, because it was finally time for potato pancakes.

Uncle Dennis served the potato pancakes. Witten looked at the plates on the table, and was confused. Uncle Dennis was serving everyone frozen waffles hot out of the toaster.

"These? These are potato pancakes?" Witten asked. His uncle stared at him, shooting back a look so vicious it reminded Witten of the night he met Brush Cutter in his dream.

"Stop talking. Eat!" a grumpy Uncle Dennis hissed.

Grandma Becky started to laugh. She laughed so hard she fell out of her chair, sending 'potato pancakes' flying onto the deck. Margo and Montana rushed to the deck, grabbed a couple 'pancakes' and bolted off. Soon everyone was laughing about potato pancakes. Everyone except Uncle Dennis!

13

Unlocking The Secret

"Okay, I'm done," Witten mumbled, his cheeks packed with food.

"Me too, let's go," Kannon chimed in, still chewing his breakfast. He pushed back his chair and stood up. The grownups hadn't even had time to pour syrup on their 'potato pancake' waffles, but the boys were ready to head back to the treasure chest. They wanted to pop open the box and see if it was Brush Cutter's treasure.

"Wait just a minute," Papa said. "What do you say?"

"May we be excused?" both boys chimed in at the same time as crumbs of food flew out of their mouths. They moved to the edge of the deck without waiting for an answer. There was no way the grownups were going to keep them away from their treasure any longer.

The brothers raced off the deck onto the steep gravel path that led toward the old wooden box. They knelt beside it, trying to figure out how to open it. Kannon tugged and pulled on the rusty lock, but it wouldn't give way. After being buried underground for so many years it was locked tight. Witten picked up a rock, gave the lock a few whacks, and tried with all his might to smash the lock open.

"Hey guys, take it easy!" Papa yelled from the deck. "Uncle Joe is coming down to help you."

Uncle Joe trotted down the hill, looking like a real construction worker. He was wearing a brown leather tool belt with a hammer and screwdriver hanging from it. His coffee was in one hand, a huge sledgehammer in the other, and a big smile covered his face.

"Let's take a look," he told the boys. "Hand me that screwdriver. We'll do this nice and easy." Uncle Joe held the tip of the screwdriver where the metal loop entered the lock. He tapped the screwdriver handle with the hammer, carefully trying to find the easiest way to open the trunk. By now Grandma Becky, Papa, Uncle Dennis, and the dogs had all gathered around the box.

"I can get it," Witten yelled. He took a step toward the box, then swung the sledgehammer at the lock near Uncle Joe's fingers. *WHAM!* Uncle Joe moved his hands just before Witten's mighty swing smashed the lock. The hit sent the tools and Witten flying across the lawn! But the lock didn't open.

"What are you doing?" Uncle Joe hollered. "You almost killed me! Put that thing down!"

When the sledgehammer smashed the treasure chest, Grandma Becky and Papa hollered at Witten. Kannon knew that his brother was going to to be grounded for life! Suddenly a shout interrupted the chaos.

"Look, it moved!" Uncle Dennis hollered. "The lock, it moved!"

Everyone stared. The sledgehammer smash had moved the lock slightly! A bit of shiny metal was showing, and the lock was almost half open. Uncle Joe grabbed the sledgehammer and gave the lock another mighty whack.

CLICK! The lock snapped open! Uncle Joe grabbed the lock, then wiggled it until it came off of the box. He tried to pry the box lid open with the screwdriver, but the rusty hinges wouldn't move.

"Grab the hammer!" Uncle Joe commanded. Witten sprinted across the yard and retrieved the tool.

Tap! Tap, tap, tap! Each hit on the screwdriver moved the lid slightly. *Tap, tap!* Uncle Joe kept working, moving the screwdriver around the box and prying at the lid. Suddenly it popped and Uncle Joe pulled the lid with a steady grip. The hinges groaned, the lid gave way, and the treasure chest finally opened.

There it was at last! Inside the wooden box, they all saw the treasure that the brothers had searched so hard to find.

14

The Treasure Of Raft Island

*C*AW, CAW, CAW! THE crows squawking on the beach made the only sound. Everyone was silent as they huddled together over the open treasure chest. They were stunned at what they saw. The old chest was packed with all the treasures of Raft Island.

"YAHOO, we found it!" Kannon screamed.

"We're RICH!" Witten hollered. He and his brother grabbed each other and started jumping around the yard. One quick look into the box had let them know their treasure hunt had been a success. They had found the hidden treasure of Brush Cutter the pirate, and now it was theirs!

The treasure chest was packed to the brim. The boys stopped jumping and crouched down near the edge of the box. They started helping Uncle Joe pick the treasures out one at a time.

Brush Cutter had packed an amazing collection into the treasure chest. There were coins that the brothers were sure Brush Cutter had stolen from ships before he set them on fire. Surprisingly, the chest held much more than just money. Brush Cutter had packed the treasure chest with lots of everyday things they had seen on the Raft Island beach. Why did the famous pirate put those things in the chest?

They carefully pulled each item out, looked it over and set it on the grass. The boys stacked the coins into a big pile on the lawn between them. "We'll split it all," Kannon told his brother. "Half for me, half for you."

"What about half for me and Papa?" Grandma Becky asked. She was the world's best at finding good deals lying around. Everyone knew that this box full of free money was just too good of a deal for Grandma Becky to pass up.

"Go dig up your own!" Uncle Dennis joked. Kannon was sure Grandma Becky was going to pick up the shovel and start digging. But she just laughed and smiled as she watched the boys unpack their treasure.

There were shells inside the chest, different types that the boys recognized from their walks in the mud with Uncle Joe. There were clam, oyster, and moon snail shells. Many were painted in beautiful colors. Inside one shell they found an old photo, a picture of smiling big woman with a parrot beside her.

"Beluga. It's Beluga—I recognize her. That *was* her on the deck!" Kannon exclaimed.

There were also sand dollars tucked among the real money. Witten remembered seeing all the sand dollars in his dream the night he and Margo went to the beach in front of Brush Cutter's house. There were also beautiful rocks, a crab shell and some small pieces of driftwood in the box.

"Why did he put all this junk in there?" Witten wanted to know.

Suddenly Margo and Montana lunged at the box. They stuck their heads inside and pulled out two rawhide dog bones. The happy dogs trotted away, ready to chew and play keep away with one another for the rest of the day.

"I bet Brush Cutter put those bones in there for his fierce dog in the tree house!" Kannon exclaimed.

Witten pulled out a small book named *Raft Island Treasure Hunters*. Attached to the bottom of the book was a folded piece of paper. It had burn marks along one side. The boys recognized it immediately.

"The map! It's the other side of Brush Cutter's treasure map!" they yelled.

It was the other half of the map that they had found in the bottle on the beach. It had a big, black X right near a drawing of some caves! Fred Stinger had been right—Brush Cutter was hiding the treasure chest when Stinger saw him at the cave!

"Look, there's something on the back," Kannon said. "It's writing." The writing on the back of the map was faded and hard to read. The boys handed it to Papa to read.

"It's a message," he said. "It looks like it was written for whoever found this treasure." Then Papa began to read:

This Pirate's Life

Yo, Ho, Ho! And a bottle of rum,
This pirate's life has been full of fun.
But listen-up Mates and it'll be clear
Why this pirate put these treasures here.

A pirate sails for money all his life,
Raiding ships for loot on a summer night.
But it's more than cash that makes his life good,
It's having friends like you visit
his neighborhood!

'Cuz seeing mud, getting shells and
spending time
Are worth more to a pirate
than a ship full of dimes.
With two good dogs and great friends like you,
Raft Island is very rich in fun things to do!

So remember this, our hearty Mates,
Keep your treasure of friends in a special place.
And Raft Island's riches you'll see as you look,
At the bottom of this chest--
hidden under the book!

The boys looked at each other. Kannon quickly reached into the treasure chest and slid his hand along the bottom. At one end he discovered a small wooden knob. He gave the knob a tug. And slowly the bottom of the treasure chest began to slide up towards him.

Carefully he lifted the fake bottom of the chest into his hands. With Witten huddled by his side, he looked at the wood. "Turn it over!" Witten urged. When Kannon did, they discovered a magic window on the other side. The boys peered into that window and discovered the real treasure of Raft Island.

In the magic window two happy faces stared right back at them. It was a mirror, and in it they saw the reflection of the greatest treasure hunters to ever visit Raft Island. The brothers smiled, and they understood. This was the special treasure that made Raft Island a rich and magical place. The treasure that turned Raft Island into a magical place for Uncle Joe and Uncle Dennis, and for everyone who visited them on Raft Island.

They were the treasure! Their happy, smiling faces were the great treasures of Raft Island! The brothers gave each other a big hug, and then they saw something else in the magic window.

There was another reflection in the window behind them. It was Grandma Becky. She was standing behind them, admiring the beauty and richness of the special treasures of Raft Island. And Grandma Becky was crying.

And that, my friend, is the end of the story.

Acknowledgements

The inspiration for this story came from two brothers who visited Raft Island on a family vacation. During the vacation, their uncles created a treasure hunt that involved the activities described in this book. My thanks to Ian, Nolan, Betty and Dan for making this tale possible. They were the original Raft Island Treasure Hunters. Not only did they have a successful treasure hunt, but I also struck it rich "Once Upon a Time" four decades ago when our friendship began.

Deep appreciation goes to both Mazie Quinn and Joe Sanchez for their help developing the story. Their assistance with ideas, encouragement, and editing chores helped make this book a reality.

I am also grateful to Richard Lehman for the illustrations he crafted. A talented artist and long-time friend, I have had the pleasure of working with him to illustrate many writing projects over the years.

A big shout out also goes to the Pierce County, Washington road crews. Those big orange "BRUSH CUTTER AHEAD" warning signs you post along the roads do more than just keep us safe. They keep the magnificent legend of the pirate Brush Cutter alive for generations to come.

About the Author

DJ Quinn, Author

DJ Quinn is the second of nine children raised in Helena, Montana. He currently resides in Gig Harbor, WA, the area used as the setting for **Raft Island Treasure Hunters**. Quinn is also the author of **Stick Figures: A Big Brother Remembers**, a memoir of his Big Brothers match with a handicapped boy.

Follow DJ Quinn at https://www.DJQuinnAuthor.com

About the Illustrator

Richard Lehman

    Artist Richard Lehman is a life-long Seattle resident, and currently resides in the city's Madison Park area. His work has been published in a variety of media, including children's books, magazines, newspapers and national labor union publications. A long-time contributor to his community's *Madison Park Times*, Lehman uses his humor and artistic magic to capture unique perspectives of the beauty and absurdities that all of us encounter in our daily lives.

Also by DJ Quinn

Stick Figures: A Big Brother Remembers

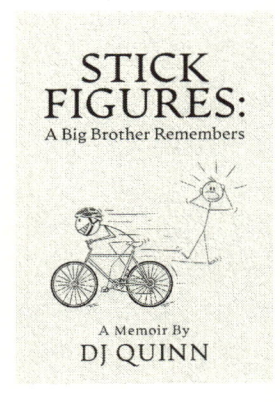

"Spend a couple hours a week with a kid, that's all it takes." How hard could that be? 'Big Brother' DJ Quinn would soon find out. His new 'Little Brother' Mike, an energetic 7-year-old burdened with disabilities, was ready for adventure. A unique friendship evolved, crafted by shared time and talks of Santa, God, showgirls and speech therapy.

In his debut memoir *Stick Figures: A Big Brother Remembers*, Quinn takes you along to share an intimate view of an epic 13-year journey. A true story told with compassion and humor, *Stick Figures* touches readers' hearts as they experience the joys, courage, hopes, and heartbreaks the two Brothers encounter.

Stick Figures: A Big Brother Remembers
Available at: **www.DJQuinnAuthor.com**

Made in the USA
Middletown, DE
13 April 2024